THE
MONSTER
BED

SO HE DID IT INSTEAD!

He laid himself down and he shivered with fright.
He wished that his mummy could kiss him
    goodnight
And check that no monsters were under his bed.
But she wasn't there...

And feeling so tired he could wander no more
He stopped at the cave and he went through
    the door.
He saw the bare mattress, and desperate for rest
He peeled off his wellies and stripped to his vest.

So there Dennis lay, staring up at the springs,
Thinking of birthdays and chocolate and things.

Now a certain small boy who played truant
    from school
Got lost in the wood, in the dark – little fool!

"Please take off my pillow and blankets," he said,
"From now on, I'd rather sleep under my bed,
For if I am there and a human comes near
It won't think to look for me, safe under here."

But when she bent down to kiss Dennis, he chose
To fasten his fangs round her warty old nose.
He tied up his toes in a knot round her knees.
"Led go of be, Deddid, you're hurtig be, please!"
"Only," he said, "if you help with my plan."
"All right,"squealed his mummy, "I will if I can."

"Oh, no," said his mummy, "I cannot agree,
There are no human beings, what fiddle-dee-fee
They are only in stories. They do not exist.
Now get into bed and be quiet and kissed."

"But why?" asked his mummy. "There's
   nothing to fear,
I've given you teddy, the light switch is here."
"The humans will get me," cried Dennis.
   "They'll creep
Under my monster bed, when I'm asleep."

Now Dennis the monster was mostly polite;
He tried very hard not to bellow and bite,
Except, I'm afraid, when the time came for bed.
"I'm frightened! I'm frightened!" the wee
    monster said.

Oh, never go down there, unless you are brave.
In case you discover the Cobbeldy Cave.
For inside that cave which is gloomy and glum
Live Dennis the monster and Dennis's mum.

Never go down to the Withering Wood,
The goblins and ghoulies are up to no good.
The gnomes are all nasty, the trolls are all hairy.
And even the pixies and fairies are scary.

THE
MONSTER
BED

Jeanne Willis · Susan Varley

Mini Treasures

RED FOX

1 3 5 7 9 0 8 6 4 2

Copyright © text Jeanne Willis 1986
Copyright © illustrations Susan Varley 1986

Jeanne Willis and Susan Varley have asserted their rights
under the Copyright, Designs and Patents Act, 1988
to be identified as the author and illustrator of this work.

First published in the United Kingdom 1986 by Andersen Press

First published in Mini Treasures edition 1998
by Red Fox,
Random House, 20 Vauxhall Bridge Road,
London, SW1V 2SA

Random House Australia (Pty) Ltd
20 Alfred Street, Milsons Point, Sydney,
New South Wales 2061, Australia

Random House New Zealand Limited
18 Poland Road, Glenfield,
Auckland 10, New Zealand

Random House South Africa
PO Box 2263, Rosebank 2121, South Africa

RANDOM HOUSE UK Limited Reg No. 954009

A CIP catalogue record for this book
is available from the British library.
Printed in Singapore

ISBN 0 099 26345 9